CLOWNS ON VACATION

Nina Laden

Walker & Company   New York

Children of all ages
And Ladies and Gentlemen,
This is the book
That answers the question:
When the circus is over,
After the standing ovation,
What do clowns do
When they go on vacation?

Do they change their clothes
And clean their faces?

Do they pack a trunk
Or a few suitcases?

Somewhere cold?

How do they get there?
By land?

Along the way,
Where do they stay?

In a fancy hotel
Or a bad one that smells?

Do they pay lots of rent
Or sleep in a tent?

Do clowns like the beach?

Or do clowns like a pool?

Do they play in the sand
Or read in the shade?

Can clowns get a tan
And drink lemonade?

When clowns get hungry,
What do they eat?
Something juicy?
Something sweet?
What's a clown's favorite treat?

If they get tired of the sun
And want to have fun
Do they take in the sights

And scale the heights?

What if clowns get lost
Or miss a connection,
Are they too proud to stop
And ask for directions?

Or do they have adventures

And find hidden treasures?

Do clowns take photos

And buy odds and ends?

Do they send postcards
To all of their friends?

But when it's time to stop,
Will they go back to the Big Top?

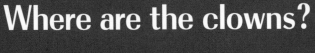

The crowd is waiting.
The Ringmaster frowns.
Children, Ladies, and Gentlemen!
Wait,
Where are the clowns?

Don't Miss the Circus!

Did they miss their plane?
Did they lose their luggage?
Who is to blame?

Ah, here they come,
On the run,
Your favorite sensation,
Doing what clowns do
When they're not on vacation!

For Col. Harry & Sally Buckley,
my father- and mother-in-love.
Family is the real treasure.

First published in the United States of America in 2002 by
Walker Publishing Company, Inc.

Published simultaneously in Canada by Fitzhenry and Whiteside, Markham, Ontario L3R 4T8

For information about permission to reproduce selections from
this book, write to Permissions, Walker & Company, 435 Hudson Street, New York, New York 10014

Library of Congress Cataloging-in-Publication Data

Laden, Nina.
Clowns on vacation / written and illustrated by Nina Laden.
p. cm.
Summary: A family of clowns and their dog pack up the elephant and go on a vacation.
ISBN 0-8027-8780-0 -- ISBN 0-8027-8781-9 (RE)
[1. Clowns--Fiction. 2. Vacations--Fiction. 3. Stories in rhyme.] I. Title.

PZ8.3.L125 Cl 2001
[E]--dc21   2001046583

The illustrations for this book
were created in gouache and photomontage.

Book design by Victoria Allen

Visit Walker & Company's Web site at www.walkerbooks.com

Printed in Hong Kong

2 4 6 8 10 9 7 5 3 1